With thanks to my two guinea pigs ...
Hannah and **Ellie**

First published 2005 by **W**alker Books Ltd
87 Vaux**h**all Walk, London SE11 5HJ

This edition published 2006

10 9 8 7 6 5 4

Text and illustr**a**tions © 2005 William Bee

www.williambee.com

The righ**t** of William Bee to be identified as author/illustrator of this work
has been asserted by him in accordance with the Copyright, Designs and Patents Act 1988

This book has been typ**e**set in Frutiger

Printed in China

British Library Cataloguing in Publication Data: a catalogue record
for this book is available from the B**r**itish Library

ISBN 978-1-4063-0133-5

www.walkerbooks.co.uk

whatever

by william bee

WALKER BOOKS
AND SUBSIDIARIES
LONDON • BOSTON • SYDNEY • AUCKLAND

This is Billy.

And this is Billy's dad.

Billy can be very difficult to please.

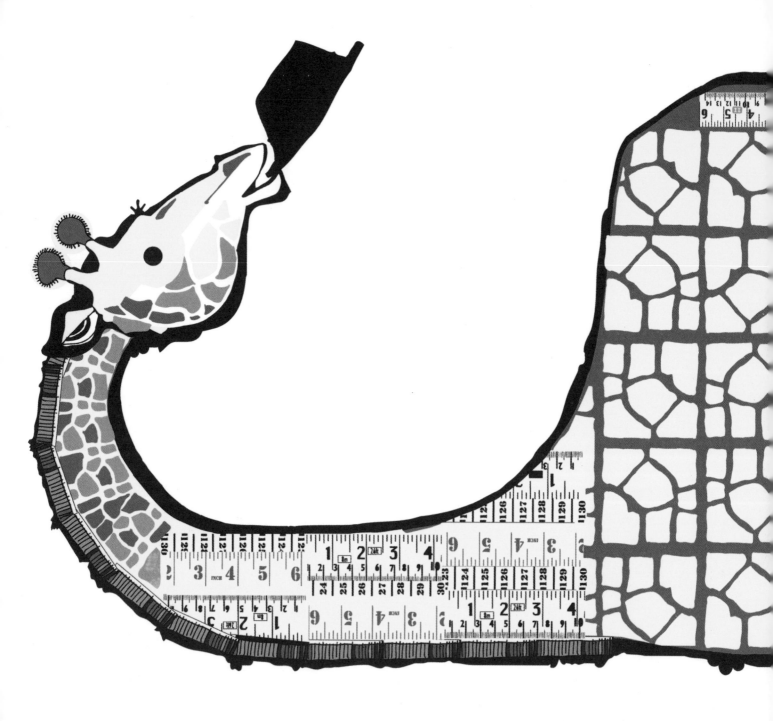

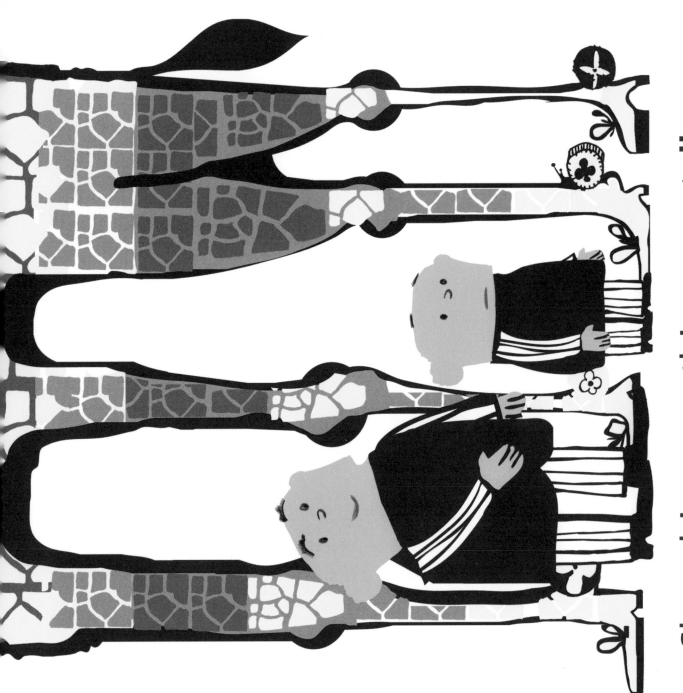

Show him something very tall ...

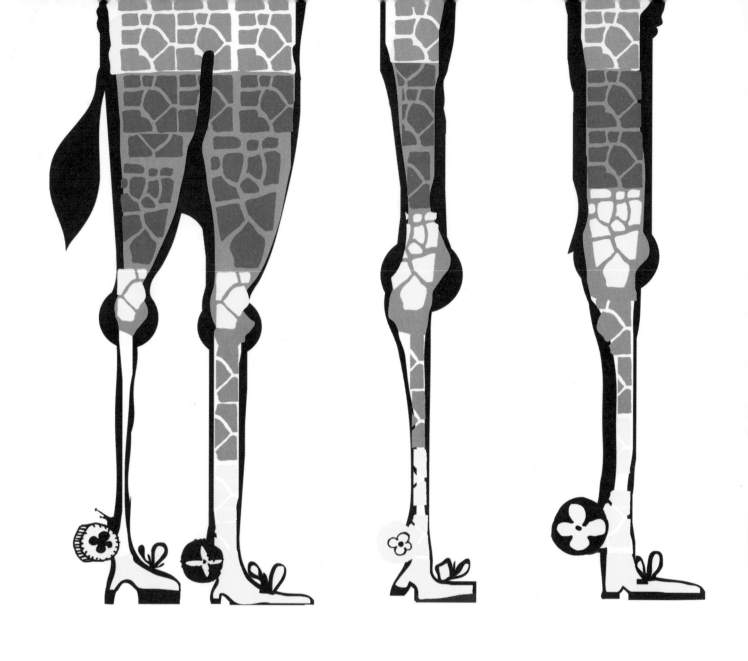

and he'll say **"…whatever."**

Show him something very **small** …

and he'll say "...whatever."

Play him a tune on the world's **curliest** trumpet … and he'll say …

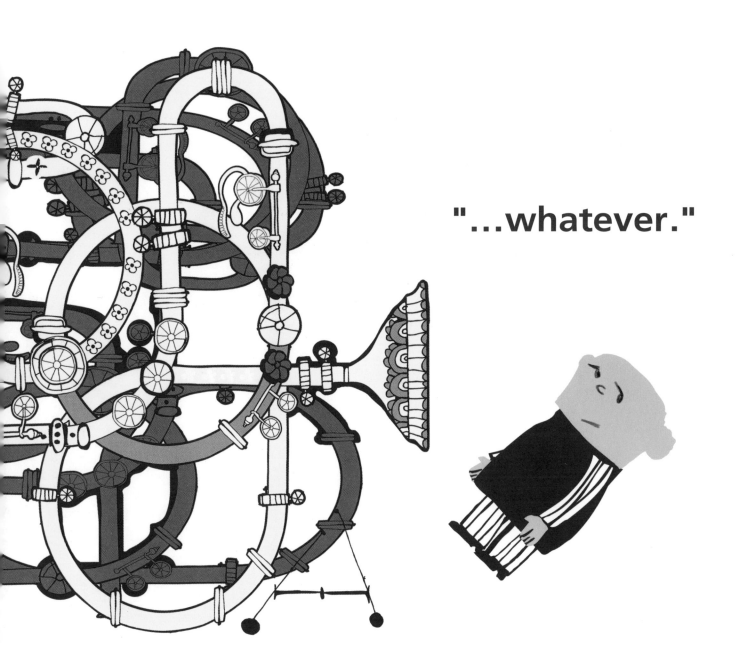

Bounce him off the world's **bounciest** castle … and he'll say …

"...whatever."

Take him for a ride on the world's **steamiest** train … and he'll say …

"...whatever."

Fly him to the edge of outer space ...
and he'll say ...

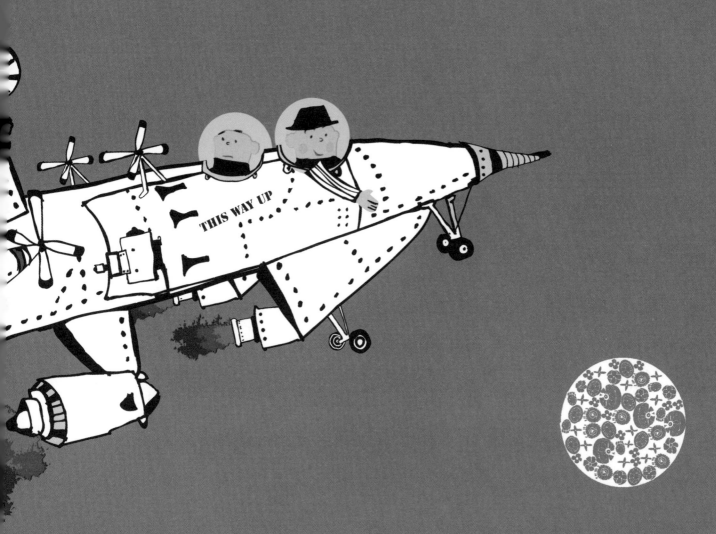

"...whatever."

And, when you try and scare him with the world's **hungriest** tiger ... he'll say ...

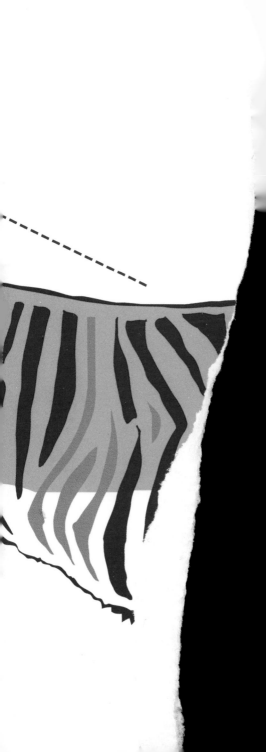

...whatever."

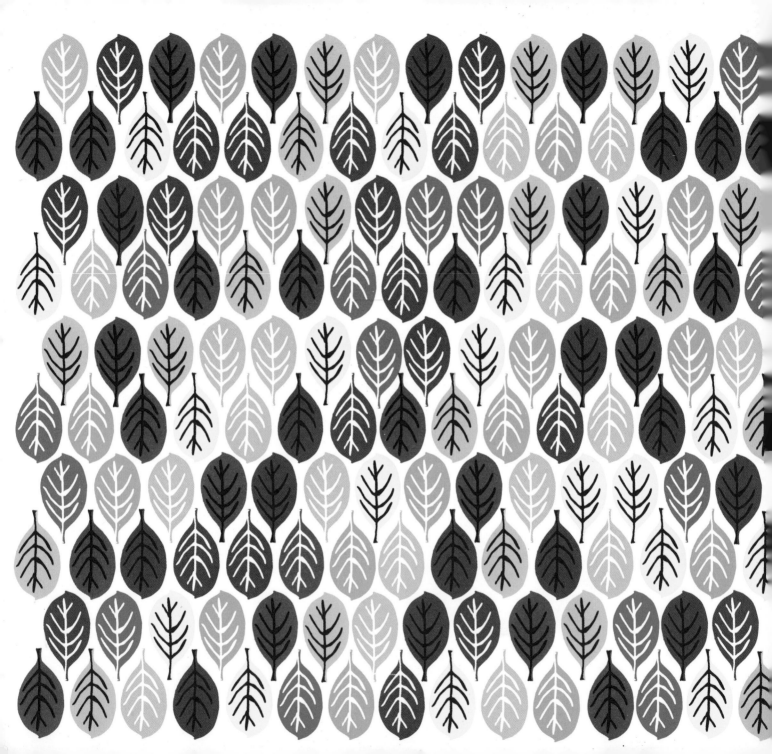